WILLIS

BY JAMES MARSHALL

HOUGHTON MIFFLIN COMPANY BOSTON

www.houghtonmifflinbooks.com

Library of Congress Cataloging in Publication Data

Marshall, James, 1942–1992

Willis.

Summary: Snake, Bird, and Lobster use their imagination to earn twenty-nine cents to buy sunglasses for their friend Willis.

[1. Friendship—Fiction] I. Title.

PZ7.M35672Wi   [Fic]   74-5259

RNF ISBN 0-618-12441-1 PAP ISBN 0-618-12442-X

Printed in Singapore

TWP 10 9 8 7 6 5 4 3

For

EVA KNOX EVANS

and

JOHN MITZEL

Not so very long ago, on the most beautiful beach in the world, there sat a most unhappy creature. His name was Willis, and all summer long, large salty tears rolled down his cheeks and dropped into the sand.

One afternoon, three strangers appeared from behind a large dune.

"My goodness!" exclaimed Bird. "Don't you look unhappy!"

"I'd rather not talk about it," said Willis, sniffing into his handkerchief.

"Oh, tell us what's the matter," begged Bird.

"Yes, do," said Lobster, who promptly dozed off.

"Well," said Willis timidly, "if you really want to know, I am unhappy because I haven't any sunglasses. Wonderful things are happening on the beach, but the sun is so bright I can barely open my eyes. I'm missing all the fun."

"Then, as I see it," said Bird, "all you have to do is buy a pair of sunglasses, and things will be fine."

"But sunglasses cost twenty-nine cents," said Willis, "and I don't have twenty-nine cents." He began to sob.

"There, there," said Snake. "No need for that. I have a dime. Why don't we buy a pair of sunglasses with my dime? I've had it for the longest time, and I've never used it."

Bird was quite put out. "Really, Snake, how can you be so dense? Don't you know that sunglasses cost twenty-nine cents? A dime is only ten cents."

"Oh," said Snake, who wasn't very good at arithmetic. "Then how much more do we need?"

"We need," said Bird in a haughty tone, "nineteen more cents. Ten cents and nineteen cents make twenty-nine cents."

"I see," said Snake. "But where shall we find nineteen cents?"

Bird scratched his beak with his wing.

"We shall work for the nineteen cents!" he announced.

"That's an idea," said Snake. "Yes, by all means, we must hurry off and find a job this very minute. We should be able to earn nineteen cents in no time at all."

"But what sort of work will we look for?" asked Willis.

"Oh, something will turn up," said Snake.

And before anyone could think of an argument, the four friends were sailing away on Bird's bicycle.

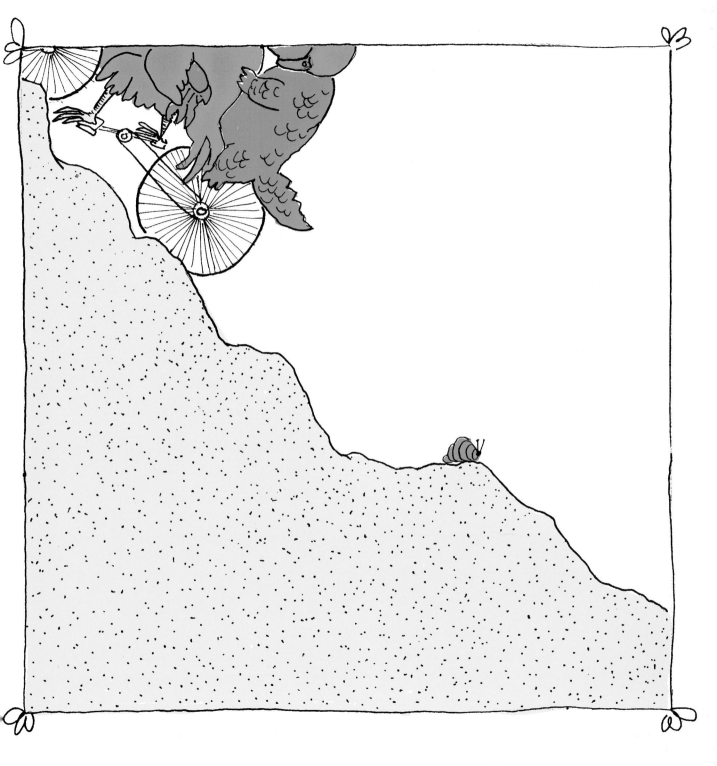

Suddenly Bird applied the brakes. "Look!" he exclaimed, pointing to a cottage beside the road. "That cottage is badly in need of paint. Why don't we spruce it up? I'm sure the owner would gladly pay us for our trouble. Surely a fresh coat of paint is worth nineteen cents."

The others thought it a splendid idea. "That Bird really knows what he is doing," whispered Snake to Willis.

Buckets of fresh paint were found in the garage.

"Let's go to work!" called Bird. And everyone went to work.

Lobster, who was, of course, still asleep, held an extra brush in his claws.

Very soon the cottage was looking quite spectacular.

But as the painters stepped back to admire their work, a small roadster pulled into the driveway, and out stepped a large rhinoceros. She was upset. "Just look what you've done to my little cottage! You've ruined it!"

"Now, now," said Snake. "We only spruced it up a bit. That will be nineteen cents please."

Rhino was outraged. "No nineteen cents from me! I ought to step on all four of you! Get out of my sight this minute! And don't forget to take that lobster with you!"

"Fussy Rhino," said Bird, when they were back on the road.

"I don't think we were cut out to be painters," said Willis.

It was not long before they came upon a large sign.

"I can't read," said Snake.

"That is not surprising," said Bird. "It says LIFEGUARDS WANTED."

"Sounds like fun," said Snake.

Following the sign's directions, they arrived at a beautiful swimming pool.

Relaxing beside the pool was a fat turtle.

"Sir," said Bird, "we would like to be your new lifeguards."

"The job doesn't pay much," snapped Turtle. "Only nineteen cents a week."

The friends were delighted. "That will be just dandy!"

"Fine," said Turtle. "Here are your swimming trunks. Put them on and go to work."

The trunks fit perfectly.

"My, don't you look grand," said Turtle. "I've never seen a more handsome bunch of lifeguards. Why don't you all go for a quick dip before the swimmers arrive?"

"Not me," said Bird.

"Oh, I just couldn't," said Willis.

"Count me out," said Snake.

"And why not?" asked Turtle.

"I don't know how to swim," said Bird.

"Neither do I," said Snake.

"I'm afraid I've forgotten," said Willis.

Lobster, of course, knew how to swim, but he was fast asleep.

Turtle was furious. "Take off those grand-looking swimming trunks this minute! How do you expect to be lifeguards if you don't know how to swim?"

"I never thought of that," said Snake.

Turtle was so angry that he jumped into the pool to cool off.

And the friends found themselves on the road once again.

"I'll never get my sunglasses," sighed Willis.

"There, there," said Snake in a soothing voice.

"Why is the ground shaking?" Bird wanted to know.

At that moment an elephant came around the bend.

"What a superb-looking crowd," he said. "Where, if I may be so bold as to ask, are you fellows going?"

"We're on our way to find a job," they explained.

"Do you like peanuts?" asked Elephant.

The friends looked at each other. What did that have to do with finding a job?

"Just answer the question," said Elephant. "Do you like peanuts or not?"

No, no one was particularly fond of peanuts.

"Smashing!" exclaimed Elephant. "It just so happens that just down the road is my very own candied peanut factory. You can work for me."

"What's the salary?" asked Bird. "We don't work for peanuts, you know."

The salary was nineteen cents, and that was just dandy.

"Now remember," said Elephant before retiring for his daily snooze, "you are not to eat so much as a single peanut!"

"We understand perfectly," said Willis.

In no time at all the friends were hard at work. Willis inspected and carefully washed each peanut. When the peanuts were dry, Snake put each one onto a tiny wooden stick. It was Bird's job to dunk the peanuts into a bowl of rich candy syrup, made from Elephant's own secret recipe.

"You know," said Snake, "I've never cared for peanuts, it's true. But candied peanuts, well, that is quite another matter. And these look especially delicious."

"They certainly do," agreed Bird. "Do you suppose we might have just one little nibble?"

"I don't see that it could hurt anything," said Willis.

When the Elephant awoke, he heard strange groanings.

"I knew it!" he cried. "They've eaten all my peanuts!"

And it was true. Not one peanut was left in the factory.

And Willis, Bird, and Snake weren't feeling well at all.

"We simply couldn't help ourselves," moaned Snake.

Elephant went to his file cabinet and took out a bottle of greenish liquid. "Lucky for you that I happen to have a bottle of my special tonic. It tastes awful, but it works."

Willis, Bird, and Snake each swallowed a large tablespoon of Elephant's tonic. It tasted awful, but it worked.

"You're fired," said Elephant.

Back on the road, everyone was unhappy.

"We'll never find a job we can do," said Snake. "We're just a bunch of good-for-nothings."

"Yes," Bird and Willis agreed, nodding their heads, "we're just a bunch of good-for-nothings."

"Now just one little minute!" exclaimed an angry voice.

"Who said that?" asked Willis.

It was Lobster. "I've never heard such talk! You ought to be ashamed of yourselves! Don't you know everyone is good for something?"

Bird pulled the bicycle over to the side of the road, and everyone listened to Lobster.

"Let me repeat myself," he said. "Everyone is good for something."

"And you will always be good at what you like to do most."

The friends were amazed. "It sounds so simple."

"It is simple," Lobster explained. "Now all we must do is decide what each of us likes to do most."

Everyone thought long and hard.

"Well," said Bird timidly, "I've never told anyone, and you may think it a bit unusual, but I like to play the cello."

No one thought it unusual in the least.

Willis spoke up next. "You may not know it to look at me," he said, "but I simply love to dance."

"You see," said Lobster, "everyone has something that he likes to do most. What about you, Snake?"

"I," announced Snake, "am a hypnotist. There is nothing I enjoy more than putting people to sleep."

"Interesting," said Lobster. "There is nothing I enjoy more than going to sleep. Perhaps you could hypnotize me?"

"Delighted," responded Snake, "but I don't see how all this will help us find the nineteen cents we need for Willis's sunglasses."

Lobster, however, had a plan.

A very fine plan indeed.

"Everyone," he explained, "likes good music. Am I right? Everyone likes fine dancing. No? And I'm sure that everyone would be terribly amused to watch Snake hypnotize me to sleep."

The others agreed that this was probably true.

"I propose," said Lobster, "that we present a talent show. We can charge a penny a ticket. Surely nineteen of our friends will be glad to come."

"Of course!" exclaimed Bird. "Why didn't I think of that?"

"But first," said Lobster, "we must build a stage. Things look so much better on a stage."

"That Lobster is even smarter than Bird," whispered Snake to Willis.

When the stage was completed, Willis and Bird rehearsed, and Lobster and Snake went about the beach passing out advertisements.

TALENT SHOW THIS AFTERNOON!! ONE PENNY.

"I'm so nervous," said Lobster. "I hope I'll be able to go to sleep for you."

"Have no fear," Snake assured him.

That afternoon crowds began to form around the stage.

A hush fell over the audience. Snake and Lobster had appeared.

Such an exciting moment! Staring into Lobster's eyes, Snake began to move back and forth, back and forth, ever so slowly.

In no time at all, Lobster was sound asleep.

The audience was amazed.

As soon as Lobster was removed from the stage, it was time for Willis and Bird to perform.

Placing his bow carefully on the strings of his cello, Bird began to produce the most beautiful music. He was very good. It was easy to see that this was what he loved to do most in the entire world.

And Willis, inspired by the lovely sounds, danced away to his heart's content. There were many cheers and much applause.

When the show was over, Bird began counting the money.

"My, my," he said over and over.

"Oh, do we have enough?" asked Snake, out of breath.

"We have more than enough," announced Bird. "We have enough to buy sunglasses for all of us!"

"Hurray!" exclaimed Willis and Snake. "And we owe it all to Lobster. Let's tell him the good news."

But Lobster didn't want to hear the good news. He was doing the one thing he enjoyed doing most. And he was very good at it, too.